Kali and Sida
FINDING HOME

This book is dedicated to those
who have committed their lives to preserving
and protecting wildlife.

M.M.

First edition December 2020

Illustrated by Oliver Kryzz Bundoc

ISBN 978-1-7774522-1-6 (hardcover)

ISBN 978-1-7774522-0-9 (paperback)

ISBN 978-1-7774522-2-3 (ebook)

www.margaretmendoza.com

Kali and Sida
FINDING HOME

by

Margaret Mendoza

Illustrated by

Oliver Kryzz Bundoc

There was once a mighty mountain named Mount Baco. On one side of the mountain, a tarsier named **Sida** lived with her family. Tarsiers are the smallest and slowest animals in the land.

On the other side of the mountain, a tamaraw named **Kali** lived with his family. Tamaraws are the fiercest and largest animals in the land.

One day, a strong typhoon swept over the mountain and separated Kali and Sida from their families.

Once the typhoon passed, Kali was alone and scared.
He remembered what his parents told him if he ever got lost.
"Find the high ground and you will be found."

Kali started running, looking for the high ground, but crashed into a bunch of bamboo trees.

When Kali looked up, he saw a small furry
animal with big eyes glaring down at him.

"Hey! Watch where you're going! You
almost knocked me out of my tree!"
the furry animal yelled.

"What are you?" inquired Kali.

"I am a tarsier and my name is Sida. We don't like loud noises and we usually sleep during the day. There are not too many of us around, so we like to keep to ourselves."

"What are you?" asked Sida.

"I am a tamaraw and my name is Kali. There are also very few of us left because everyone wants our horns and my home keeps getting destroyed. I am lost and looking for my family."

"My parents always told me, 'Find the high ground and you will be found,'" explained Kali. "Can you see any high ground from up there?"

"I can see a high ground, but it is quite far," replied Sida.

"I am also looking for my family. Can we look for them together?" asked Sida.

"Sure. Maybe we can help each other," replied Kali.

As Kali and Sida travelled across the land,
they came upon a raging river.

"Oh no! I cannot swim!" exclaimed Sida.

"That's alright. Hop onto my back
and I will carry you across," assured Kali.

Sida jumped onto Kali's back and held on tightly to one of his horns. Using Kali's strength and might, they battled the swift current and safely crossed the river.

Next, Kali and Sida came upon a large and dark cave through which they needed to pass. As they entered, Kali grew scared. "It is so dark in here. I cannot see anything," he whispered.

"Don't be afraid. I can see in the dark and I can also hear very well," assured Sida.

Suddenly, Sida spotted a small snake blocking their path.
"Shhh... don't move," she whispered to Kali.

"What do you see?" Kali whispered back.

Without making a sound, Sida grabbed the snake and tossed it aside.
"Oh, nothing," Sida chuckled, as she guided Kali out of the cave.

Finally, they came upon the deepest canyon they had ever seen. They could see the high ground on the other side. "Oh no!" Sida groaned. "How are we going to get across?"

"I have an idea!" Kali offered.

Using his powerful horns, Kali pushed and bent the bamboo trees until they fell across the canyon, creating a bridge.

"You are amazing!" shouted Sida.

Balancing carefully, Kali and Sida crossed the canyon.

When they reached the other side, Kali and
Sida began climbing towards the high ground.
"We're almost there, Kali," encouraged Sida.

"I can see something," gasped Kali.

"We made it!" exclaimed Kali,
as they stepped into the clearing.

"Our families are here!" Sida shouted joyfully.

"I would have never found my family
without your help," confided Kali.

"I am glad we became friends," sighed Sida.
"Friends always help each other."

Then, Kali and Sida heard some familiar sounds behind them.

"We're home!" cheered Kali and Sida.

Animal Profiles

(The real "Kali")

Species: Tamaraw
Diet: Herbivore (plant-eating)
Habitat: Tropical Forests

Tamaraws are one of the largest land mammals in the Philippines, with an adult weighing up to 240 kgs. They can be identified by their distinct V-shape horns and are a close relative of the domestic water buffalo known locally as the carabao. Tamaraws can only be found in Mindoro, Philippines and usually live in mixed forest and grassland, not too far from sources of water. Though naturally day animals, they have recently been found to roam at night to avoid human contact. Tamaraws are critically endangered due to poaching and destruction of their habitat. They are highly admired and their images are commonly used in flags and signs to represent fierceness and strength.

Kali was named in honor of *Kalibasib*, the only captive-bred tamaraw that lived for over 21 years at the Mts. Iglit-Baco National Park in Mindoro, Philippines.

Species: Tarsier

Diet: Carnivore (meat-eating)

Habitat: Tropical Forests

Tarsiers are one of the smallest mammals on the planet averaging only 5 inches in length. They can be found in various countries in Southeast Asia, mostly in the southern Philippines. Tarsiers generally live in trees and have a diet that includes insects, lizards and snakes. Naturally night animals, tarsiers use their unique ability to see in the dark and their sharp hearing to hunt their prey. Incredibly shy, they are extremely sensitive to bright lights, noises and human contact. Tarsiers are vulnerable to being endangered if not properly preserved and protected.

Sida was named as a short form of *Tarsiidae*, the scientific name of the tarsier.

Margaret Mendoza

Kali and Sida – Finding Home is the first book written by Margaret Mendoza, a 16-year old Filipino-Italian-Canadian. The book was inspired by her interest in protecting the environment and preserving two of the most vulnerable wildlife on the planet – the tamaraw and the tarsier, both indigenous to the Philippines. Margaret has frequently visited her father's home province of Mindoro, Philippines where one of her main characters, the tamaraw, can be exclusively found. Margaret is eager to share *Kali and Sida – Finding Home* with children from all over the world, in the hope that it will teach them the value of courage, teamwork and friendship.

Margaret loves sketching and did some of the original illustrations in the book, including the cover page. She lives in Toronto, Ontario, Canada with her parents, two older brothers and her two dogs, Tango and Juno.

Visit her website at

www.margaretmendoza.com.

Manufactured by Amazon.ca
Bolton, ON

16656766R00017